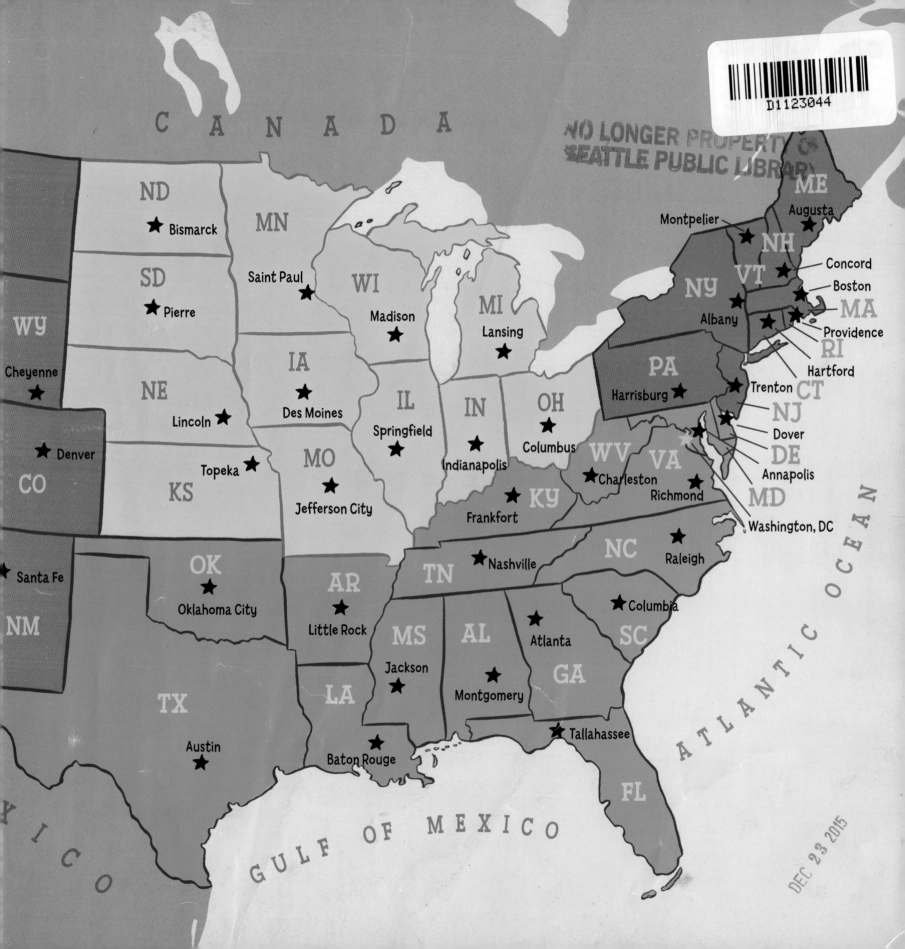

C A N A D A

ND
★ Bismarck

MN
Saint Paul ★

WI
Madison ★

MI
Lansing ★

ME
Augusta ★

Montpelier
★ NH
Concord

VT ★
NY Boston ★
MA
Albany ★ Providence
★ RI

SD
★ Pierre

WY
Cheyenne ★

NE
Lincoln ★

IA
★ Des Moines

IL
Springfield ★

IN
★ Indianapolis

OH
Columbus ★

PA
Harrisburg ★

Trenton ★ CT
NJ
Dover
DE
Annapolis
MD

Denver ★
CO

KS
Topeka ★

MO
★ Jefferson City

KY
Frankfort ★

WV VA
Charleston ★
Richmond ★
Washington, DC

Santa Fe ★

NM

OK
★ Oklahoma City

AR
★ Little Rock

TN
Nashville ★

NC
Raleigh ★

Columbia ★
SC

TX
Austin ★

LA
Baton Rouge ★

MS
Jackson ★

AL
Montgomery ★

Atlanta ★
GA

Tallahassee ★

FL

A T L A N T I C   O C E A N

G U L F   O F   M E X I C O

M E X I C O

For my puppy, Oliver

Library of Congress Cataloging-in-Publication Data is available. ISBN 978-0-06-228017-6 (trade bdg.)

The artist used line art drawn with ink on bristol and colored on an Apple MacBook Pro using Photoshop to create the artwork for this book.

Austin, Lost in AMERICA

A Geography Adventure by JEF CZEKAJ

Balzer + Bray
An Imprint of HarperCollins Publishers

Austin had grown up in a pet store. All around him, other animals were being adopted. He wanted a real home too.

And so, one night, with the help of his friends, he escaped.

For the first time ever, Austin was on his own. It was a little scary.

But he knew his home was somewhere in the United States. With the help of a trusty map, he was determined to find it!

THE NORTHEAST

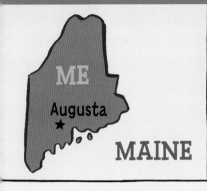

ME
Augusta ★
MAINE

Austin started his search at the easternmost point of the mainland United States, located in West Quoddy Head, Maine.

Maine produces 99% of all the blueberries in the United States.

Approximately 100 million pounds of the nation's lobsters are caught off the coast of Maine.

His lobster and blueberry allergies made him think that maybe Maine wasn't the best place for him.

So his search continued.

Montpelier
VT
VERMONT

Every year, Brattleboro, Vermont, hosts the Strolling of the Heifers, a parade of cows down its main street.

New Hampshire was a wild ride.

New Hampshire has the most roller coasters per person.

NH
Concord
NEW HAMPSHIRE

MA Boston ★

MASSACHUSETTS

In Massachusetts, a Boston terrier showed him around. There was so much good food to eat! He had a Boston cream pie (it was actually a cake). He had a Fig Newton. He had Boston baked beans. He had New England clam chowder. . . . He had a very bad stomachache.

Boston baked beans are made with navy beans, the state bean.

Its state dessert is the Boston cream pie.

Fig Newtons are named after the town of Newton, Massachusetts.

The state dog is the Boston terrier.

Maybe Massachusetts wouldn't be his home. Luckily, there were plenty more states to visit.

THE SOUTH

Tallahassee

FL

FLORIDA

Florida had to be it! It was warm. It was sunny. Austin ate oranges. He sunbathed. He swam with manatees. This would be the perfect place to live.

Florida has 663 miles of beaches.

Florida produces about 67% of the supply of oranges in the United States.

Crystal River, Florida, is one of the few places in North America where it's legal to swim with manatees.

He even got invited to a dinner party.

But when he discovered that he was to be the main course, he knew it was time to go.

The Florida Everglades is the only place in the world where alligators and crocodiles live in the same place.

Finding a home was proving to be harder than he thought. That night, Austin wished on a lone star for a clue.

AL

Montgomery ★

ALABAMA

The next morning, his quest continued.

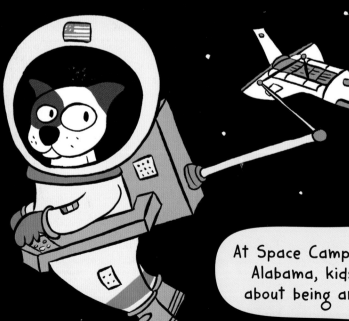

At Space Camp in Huntsville, Alabama, kids can learn about being an astronaut.

LOUISIANA

New Orleans, Louisiana, is known for its yearly Mardi Gras. People wear costumes and beads and celebrate with music and parades.

ARKANSAS

The Crater of Diamonds State Park in Pike County, Arkansas, is the only diamond-bearing place in the world where the public can dig for diamonds.

SHAKE

WAG
WAG

OKLAHOMA

Oklahoma has the highest number of strong tornadoes per square mile.

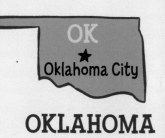

Horned Lizard Railways

Austin was discouraged but was not ready to give up. He hopped on a train heading west.

THE WEST

CALIFORNIA welcomed Austin with open paws.

CALIFORNIA

★ Sacramento

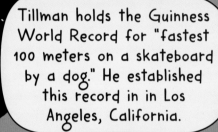

The Original Dog Beach in San Diego, California, is one of the first official leash-free beaches in the United States.

Tillman holds the Guinness World Record for "fastest 100 meters on a skateboard by a dog." He established this record in in Los Angeles, California.

LASSIE

Bosco was elected to the honorary title of "Dog Mayor" by the town of Sunol, California, in 1981.

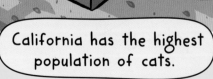
California has the highest population of cats.

To his dismay, he realized it was also a state that welcomed cats. . . .

NONCONTIGUOUS

AK

Juneau

ALASKA

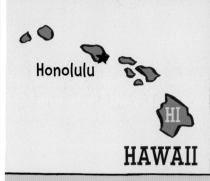

Austin finally landed in Alaska, where an Alaskan malamute was waiting to meet him. Austin could join a team of sled dogs and win the Iditarod Great Sled Race.

Honolulu

HI

HAWAII

Iolani Palace, in Honolulu, Hawaii, is the only royal palace in the United States.

Dog mushing is the official state sport of Alaska.

The noncontiguous states are the ones that do not touch any other U.S. state.

But Austin wasn't very good at pulling a sled.

WIGGLE
WIGGLE

The hula is the state dance of Hawaii.

He wasn't very good at hula dancing either. It was time to head back to the mainland.

THE MIDWEST

MI

Lansing ★

MICHIGAN

The world's only floating post office is a boat named the *J. W. Westcott II*. It delivers mail to ships as they travel through the Detroit River in Detroit, Michigan. It even has its own zip code!

MN

Saint Paul ★

MINNESOTA

The Mall of America in Bloomington, Minnesota, is the size of 84 football fields—4.87 million square feet.

WI

Madison ★

WISCONSIN

Luck, Wisconsin, is known as the yo-yo capital of the world.

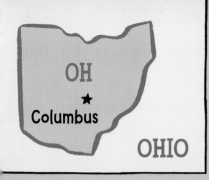

At last, Austin's journey was over! His new home had to be Ohio. A state that hosted a Banana Split Festival was the state for him.

To celebrate, he let out a loud victory howl.

Wilmington, Ohio, hosts a yearly Banana Split Festival. Many believe that the banana split was invented there.

There's a law allowing police officers in Paulding, Ohio, to bite a dog to quiet it.

As it turned out, his new home was not going to be in Ohio.

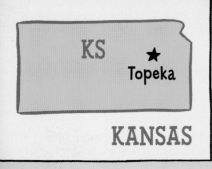

KANSAS

KS ★ Topeka

Austin was worn out. He had visited so many great states but still hadn't found his real home. He sat down in the exact center of the country to review his map.

On the map he saw something that he had never noticed before . . . his name! He was headed back to the South.

The geographic center of the contiguous United States is near Lebanon, Kansas.

TEXAS
★ Austin

"Hey, boy, you look lonely," a girl said.
"Don't you have a home? I've been
looking for a puppy just like you.
Would you like to come live with me?"

Austin wanted to.
More than anything.

In her arms, Austin realized what he'd been missing all along: a family.

He was finally home.

STATE KEY WITH CAPITALS

AK – Alaska, *Juneau*
AL – Alabama, *Montgomery*
AR – Arkansas, *Little Rock*
AZ – Arizona, *Phoenix*
CA – California, *Sacramento*
CO – Colorado, *Denver*
CT – Connecticut, *Hartford*
DE – Delaware, *Dover*
FL – Florida, *Tallahassee*
GA – Georgia, *Atlanta*
HI – Hawaii, *Honolulu*
IA – Iowa, *Des Moines*
ID – Idaho, *Boise*
IL – Illinois, *Springfield*
IN – Indiana, *Indianapolis*
KS – Kansas, *Topeka*
KY – Kentucky, *Frankfort*
LA – Louisiana, *Baton Rouge*
MA – Massachusetts, *Boston*
MD – Maryland, *Annapolis*
ME – Maine, *Augusta*
MI – Michigan, *Lansing*
MN – Minnesota, *Saint Paul*
MO – Missouri, *Jefferson City*
MS – Mississippi, *Jackson*
MT – Montana, *Helena*
NC – North Carolina, *Raleigh*
ND – North Dakota, *Bismarck*
NE – Nebraska, *Lincoln*

NH – New Hampshire, *Concord*
NJ – New Jersey, *Trenton*
NM – New Mexico, *Santa Fe*
NV – Nevada, *Carson City*
NY – New York, *Albany*
OH – Ohio, *Columbus*
OK – Oklahoma, *Oklahoma City*
OR – Oregon, *Salem*
PA – Pennsylvania, *Harrisburg*
RI – Rhode Island, *Providence*
SC – South Carolina, *Columbia*
SD – South Dakota, *Pierre*
TN – Tennessee, *Nashville*
TX – Texas, *Austin*
UT – Utah, *Salt Lake City*
VA – Virginia, *Richmond*
VT – Vermont, *Montpelier*
Washington, DC
WA – Washington, *Olympia*
WI – Wisconsin, *Madison*
WV – West Virginia, *Charleston*
WY – Wyoming, *Cheyenne*

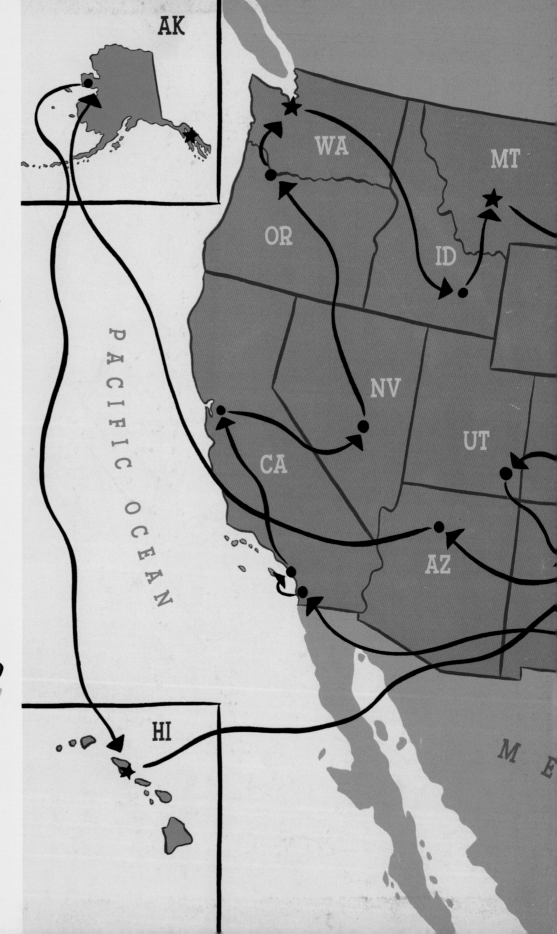